21st Century Skills **INNOVATION** *Library*

From Bats to . . . Radar

by Josh Gregory

INNOVATIONS FROM   NATURE

Published in the United States of America by Cherry Lake Publishing
Ann Arbor, Michigan
www.cherrylakepublishing.com

Content Adviser: Mariappan Jawaharlal, PhD, Professor of Mechanical Engineering, California State
Polytechnic University, Pomona, California

Design: The Design Lab

Photo Credits: Cover and page 3, ©Manamana/Shutterstock, Inc.; cover inset, ©Isselee/
Dreamstime.com; page 4, ©Catalin Petolea/Shutterstock, Inc.; page 5, ©Brian K./Shutterstock,
Inc.; page 7, ©Dreamzdesigner/Dreamstime.com; page 8, ©Ivan Kuzmin/Shutterstock, Inc.;
page 9, ©Nathape/Shutterstock, Inc.; page 10, ©tagstiles.com - Sven Gruene/Shutterstock, Inc.;
page 13, ©Ivkuzmin/Dreamstime.com; page 14, ©DIZ Muenchen GmbH, Sueddeutsche Zeitung
Photo/Alamy; page 16, ©akg-images/Alamy; page 17, ©SILBERNICUS/Alamy; page 18,
©Trinity Mirror/Mirrorpix/Alamy; page 20, ©Photos 12/Alamy; page 21, ©Don B.
Stevenson/Alamy; page 23, ©Giromin/Dreamstime.com; page 25, ©Roejoe/Dreamstime.com;
page 27, ©The Print Collector/Alamy; page 28, ©ASSOCIATED PRESS

Library of Congress Cataloging-in-Publication Data
Gregory, Josh.
 From bats to radar / by Josh Gregory.
    p. cm.—(Nature's inventors)
 Includes bibliographical references and index.
 ISBN 978-1-61080-496-7 (lib. bdg.) — ISBN 978-1-61080-583-4 (e-book) —
ISBN 978-1-61080-670-1 (pbk.)
 1. Radar—Juvenile literature. 2. Bat sounds—Juvenile literature. I. Title.
 TK6576.G74 2012
 621.3848—dc23   2012001942

Cherry Lake Publishing would like to acknowledge
the work of The Partnership for 21st Century Skills.
Please visit www.21stcenturyskills.org for more information.

Printed in the United States of America
Corporate Graphics Inc.
July 2012
CLFA11

CONTENTS

Chapter One
What Is Radar? 4

Chapter Two
Echoes in the Night Sky 9

Chapter Three
The Invention of Radar 14

Chapter Four
Further Developments 20

Chapter Five
Radar Pioneers 25

Glossary 30
For More Information 31
Index 32
About the Author 32

INNOVATIONS FROM NATURE

What Is Radar?

Have you ever shouted into an empty space to hear your voice echo?

Have you ever been in an empty room, a tunnel, or a cave and loudly shouted out "Hello"? If you have, chances are you heard your own voice coming back to you. The sound of your returning voice is called an echo. **Radar** is an amazing electronic device that locates people and objects using the principle of an echo.

The word *radar* comes from the first letters of the term "**ra**dio **d**etection **a**nd **r**anging." Radar systems work by sending out **radio waves** through the air.

Radar helps us keep track of airplanes so they do not crash into each other.

The invisible radio waves move through the air and strike an object, such as an airplane, a ship, birds, or even weather patterns such as a blizzard or a hurricane. Part of the wave is then bounced back to the radar system, where it is picked up as a radio echo.

21st Century Content

 Today, sonar is used not only to detect other vessels, but also to map the bottom of the ocean floor, locate schools of fish, find oil on land, and detect disease in humans and animals. However, radar is used much more widely. This is because sound waves do not travel as well through the air as radio waves do. Radio waves travel at the speed of light, about 186,000 miles (300,000 kilometers) per second. They also travel very long distances.

The echo then appears as an image on a screen that is part of the radar system. Using the information displayed on the screen, the radar operator can determine the location, size, shape, and how far away the object is. Radar systems can even tell how fast an object is moving.

The study of radar began in the late 19th century by German physicist Heinrich Hertz. Its use was introduced in the United States in 1925, and it became an important and effective tool for armies during World War II (1939–1945). The term *radar* was first used by U.S. Navy scientists in 1940.

Yet years before radar was put into practical use, military scientists invented a similar detection system that used **sound waves** instead of radio waves. This type of system is called **sonar**, short for "**so**und **na**vigation **r**anging." Most sonar systems send out pulses of sound, which strike an object and return to the sonar system as a sound echo. Some sonar systems send out sounds that

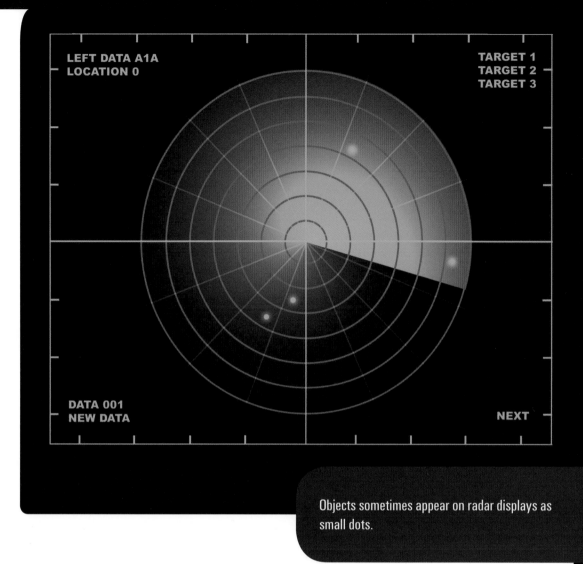

LEFT DATA A1A
LOCATION 0

TARGET 1
TARGET 2
TARGET 3

DATA 001
NEW DATA

NEXT

Objects sometimes appear on radar displays as small dots.

you can hear. Others send out sounds that are so high-pitched they cannot be heard by the human ear.

While humans have been making use of bouncing sound waves to detect objects for a very long time, there is one living creature that has been using them for much

Many species of bats use sound waves to find their way in the dark.

longer—bats. And while the earliest and most basic radar systems may have been based on bats' amazing ability to "see in the dark" through squeaks and squeals, scientists and engineers have only recently begun to understand the fine details of a bat's natural radar system. Some are even using that information to make giant leaps in our own technologies.

CHAPTER TWO

Echoes in the Night Sky

There are more than 1,100 different **species** of bats living around the world. Bats are intelligent and highly social creatures. The only places on Earth where bats do not live are the cold regions of the Arctic and Antarctica, and isolated islands. These amazing **mammals** have been on Earth for more than 50 million years. Incredibly, bats account for about one-quarter of all mammal species on Earth.

Have you ever seen a group of bats flying across the sky?

Bats vary greatly in size and appearance. The tiny bumblebee bat is the smallest species. It weighs about as much as a penny, and its wingspan is about 6.5 inches (16.5 centimeters). It is not just the smallest bat species, but also one of the smallest mammal species on Earth. The largest bat species is the flying fox bat. It is named for its foxlike face. This bat can weigh as much as 3 pounds (1.4 kilograms), and it has a wingspan that can reach 6 feet (1.8 meters).

Some bat species survive by eating fruit or other plants, but most species hunt and eat insects. About 70 percent of

Flying foxes are large, fruit-eating bats.

all bat species eat mostly insects. Some of these bats can eat up to 600 insects per hour. While searching for their **prey**, they must make sure they don't become food for larger animals such as hawks, snakes, owls, or raccoons. In addition, as the bats speed through the sky, they must avoid obstacles such as trees or power lines.

Bats are **nocturnal**. They are active and hunt only at night. To find food and avoid danger in the dark, more than half of all bat species rely on a special, built-in ability called **echolocation**. Echolocation is a type of sonar that doesn't require electronic equipment.

As a bat flies, it makes sounds. Most are too high-pitched for people to hear. The sound waves bounce off objects and then return to the bat. The bat processes the information to build a mental picture of everything around it. Bat experts have learned that a bat's relatively large ears are complex structures with a variety of ridges, grooves, and flaps. These apparently help a bat to filter and organize noises with amazing efficiency. Engineers are studying the ears much more closely now, with the hope of designing devices that can perform the same functions.

Bats have been using echolocation for millions of years. Over that time, some insects have developed natural defenses against bats. Some moths, for example,

Learning & Innovation Skills

 Bats are unique in many ways. Because they can fly, you might think they're related to birds. Bats, however, are mammals. They are warm-blooded, have hair, give birth to live babies, and nurse their babies with milk. They are the only type of mammal that can fly. Bats might seem to have a lot in common with other flying animals, but they are actually more closely related to humans or monkeys.

are covered in a powderlike substance that absorbs sound waves. This prevents the waves from echoing to the bat. A species of tiger moth escapes bats by "jamming" a bat's echolocation with a high-pitched clicking sound. One species of katydid, a type of cricket, avoids becoming a bat's dinner by stopping its mating calls when it hears the echolocation sounds of a bat in the area. These types of defense mechanisms help many insect species survive a bat's sonar abilities.

A bat emits sound waves through its odd-looking nose and receives them with its huge ears.

CHAPTER THREE

The Invention of Radar

Heinrich Hertz's discoveries helped lead to the creation of radar.

The first steps in the invention of radar were made between 1885 and 1889, when Heinrich Hertz became the first person to **broadcast** and receive radio waves. Hertz carefully studied how the waves behaved under different conditions, and realized that they acted much like light and heat waves. He also determined that radio waves could be **reflected** off surfaces.

In the following years, scientists continued to experiment with radio waves. Many of them focused on using the waves to send messages over long distances. One of the most important pioneers in this field was the Italian physicist Guglielmo Marconi. During his experiments using radio waves as a communications device, he realized that the waves could be used for other purposes as well. In 1922, he wrote a paper detailing his idea for installing radio wave broadcasting equipment on ships so that waves could be sent out to detect other vessels or objects in fog or bad weather. Humans were copying a bat's ability to substitute sound for sight when visibility is low.

Almost immediately, scientists in the United States, Great Britain, Germany, the Soviet Union, and several other countries began researching the potential uses of radio waves. The United States made its earliest discovery in 1922 at the U.S. Naval Research Laboratory (NRL) in Washington, D.C. As researchers were attempting to send a radio message across the Potomac River, a ship happened to pass between the broadcasting source and the receiver that was to pick up the echo. The researchers noticed a change in the radio signal when the ship moved in front of it. Naval researchers were excited to pursue this discovery, but military leaders were not interested in doing so at the time.

About eight years later, researchers at the NRL conducted an experiment in which an airplane flew through the path of a radio broadcasting antenna that was pointing toward the sky. Once again, they noticed that the craft produced a distinct change in the radio waves.

By the early 1930s, tensions were beginning to build between many European nations. Fearing that war would break out soon, the British military began research that would allow it to locate incoming enemy airplanes. One early device was designed to pick up sound waves from

The British military hoped to prevent attacks from enemy aircraft like the German plane pictured here.

Only after the failure of early experiments did British scientists develop radar devices such as the one pictured above.

approaching planes. Highly sensitive microphones were pointed into the sky so that operators would be able to hear the planes coming from far away. However, as researchers performed their tests, a loud truck happened to drive past on a nearby road. The microphones picked up the truck's noise, which drowned out the sound of the test airplane that was passing overhead. Military leaders

Robert Alexander Watson-Watt secured a British patent for his radar system.

called for researchers to begin searching for different methods of detecting enemy aircraft.

About the same time, Scottish physicist Sir Robert Alexander Watson-Watt was conducting research to determine how airplane pilots could use radio waves to detect nearby storms. After the British military announced its need for an airplane detection system, it occurred to Watson-Watt that radio waves could be used to detect airplanes just as well as they could detect storms. In February 1935, he wrote a paper detailing how radio waves could be reflected off airplanes. The British military was impressed, and Watson-Watt was asked to give a demonstration of his technology. His demonstration was a success, and in April 1935, he received a **patent** for his groundbreaking invention. Watson-Watt continued improving his invention, and several months later, it was able to reliably detect airplanes from about 90 miles (145 km) away. At the time, few people realized how important radar was to become.

Learning & Innovation Skills

Once scientists discovered that radio waves could be bounced off a variety of surfaces, they began applying this principle to different projects. In 1924, British physicist Sir Edward V. Appleton was attempting to prove the existence of a layer of Earth's upper atmosphere. In his experiment, he directed radio waves at the atmosphere to see if the layer would reflect them. Sure enough, the sound waves were reflected. By measuring the time it took for the waves to bounce back, he was able to determine exactly how high up the layer was. Appleton had proven the existence of the ionosphere. For his work, which led to the development of radar, he was awarded the Nobel Prize in Physics in 1947.

CHAPTER FOUR

Further Developments

Allied radar operators worked through World War II to prevent attacks from the Axis powers.

Radar technology advanced rapidly during the 1930s and 1940s, as the world's most powerful militaries began to see its potential uses. During World War II (1939–1945), the Axis powers—Germany, Japan, and their allies— fought against the Allies, made up of the United States, Great Britain, the Soviet Union, and many other nations. At the beginning of the war,

Radar is an important tool for air traffic controllers.

Germany's radar systems were the most advanced in the world. The United States and the Soviet Union had also developed effective radar technology.

Today, radar is used for more than detecting enemy planes and ships. One of radar's most important uses is for air traffic control. Air traffic controllers are in charge of observing the skies and directing flights to ensure that

Life & Career Skills

Soon after World War II began, Germany fell from its top position in the race for better radar equipment. Its leaders stopped all radar research in 1940, believing that Germany was already close to victory. The war, however, continued to rage on. By the time Germany realized its error, the United States and Great Britain had developed superior radar technology. Radar helped the Allies defeat the Axis powers. It warned the Allies of incoming planes, and radar-equipped airplanes flying over bodies of water were able to detect enemy submarines.

airplanes do not crash into each other. They use radar to keep an eye on each airplane's position in the sky. This information allows them to instruct pilots when it is safe to take off and land, or if they need to alter their flight patterns.

Similarly, radar and sonar are used to prevent boats and ships from crashing into each other. This was one of radar's earliest purposes and continues to be a major use for the technology. Experts believe that ship crashes have been reduced by as much as 90 percent since the invention of radar.

Another early function of radar still in use today is weather prediction. While older radar systems helped airplanes and ships avoid nearby storms, today's weather radar systems are much more sophisticated. They can track the movements of storm systems and predict their behavior days or even weeks ahead of time.

Radar systems have even played a role in space exploration. They can be used to track the movements of objects in space such as asteroids. Radar systems attached to satellites or space shuttles can be used to create maps of the surfaces of faraway moons and planets.

Biomimicry is one of the most rapidly expanding scientific fields. Engineers are paying closer attention to bats and their built-in radar system than ever before. They have already performed countless experiments with live bats. These experiments have taught us that bats send out a surprisingly wide range of sounds. The bats are able to translate these sounds into a detailed "audio language"

Modern radar systems help us predict and prepare for dangerous weather.

when they bounce back. As our understanding of this ability grows, we are better able to improve our own technologies.

One such example is a small flying machine known as a micro-aerial vehicle (or MAV). It can send and receive audio signals and then process them in a distinctly bat-like manner. It has also been built to look like a bat. It requires very little energy to stay in the air and refreshes that energy through wind and solar power. It can detect dangerous chemicals, making it particularly valuable to the military.

Engineers are also fitting robots with bat-inspired radar devices to prevent them from becoming damaged or destroyed in accidents. Even with modern technology, most robots have very limited visual capability. They have even poorer skill in recognizing the things they can see.

In the future, engineers are hoping to use the principles of bat echolocation to make improvements with hearing aids, sensory equipment for the blind, automotive safety, and medical equipment.

Since their invention in the early 1900s, sonar and radar technology have become a major part of our lives. Yet it's easy to forget just how incredible these discoveries are—and how incredible it is that bats have been using similar natural technologies for millions of years.

CHAPTER FIVE

Radar Pioneers

Many scientists, researchers, and inventors contributed to the invention and development of radar technology. Here are just a few of them:

Nikola Tesla (1856–1943) is one of the most famous inventors in history. He made many important discoveries relating to electricity, magnetism, and radios. Tesla was born in what was then the nation of Austria-Hungary and

Today, a statue of Tesla stands at Niagara Falls, where he helped build a hydroelectric power plant.

Life & Career Skills

Robert Rines was one of the most successful inventors of his time. At the time of his death, he held more than 80 patents. After World War II, Rines attended law school at Georgetown University and became a patent attorney. He used his skills to defend the rights of other inventors while continuing to make his own scientific discoveries. In addition to his work as a lawyer and a scientist, Rines wrote music for several Broadway and off-Broadway shows.

moved to the United States in 1884. His earliest inventions involved the construction of electric motors. In 1891, he invented a device known as the Tesla coil, which is used to produce electricity. It is found in many modern electrical devices, including televisions and radios. During World War I, Tesla became one of the first people to suggest that energy waves could be used to locate submarines. While this idea would not become a reality until years later, he was one of the first to propose its possibility.

Lawrence A. Hyland

(1897–1989) was working at the U.S. Naval Research Laboratory in 1930 when he and other researchers discovered that an airplane flying over their radio antenna caused changes in the signals they received. Further experiments by Hyland and his fellow researchers proved that radar could not only detect

By the beginning of World War I, submarines had become an important part of many countries' navies.

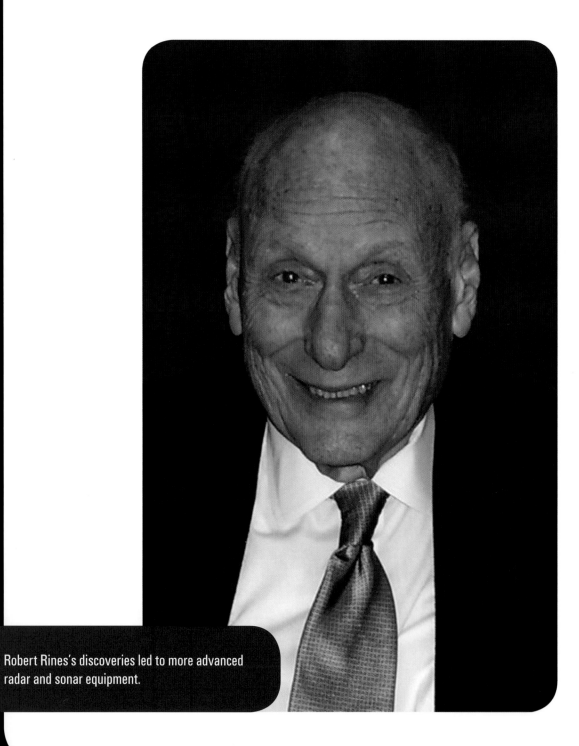

Robert Rines's discoveries led to more advanced radar and sonar equipment.

nearby airplanes, but could also be used to find out exactly where they were in the sky. In 1934, Hyland and two of his colleagues received the first U.S. patent for radar technology.

Robert H. Rines (1922–2009) was born in Boston, Massachusetts, and received a physics degree from the Massachusetts Institute of Technology before joining the U.S. Army during World War II. During the war, he helped the military develop powerful new radar systems that could display more detailed information than previous ones had. His discoveries were put to use in many other inventions, including sonar systems used to find shipwrecks and devices used to detect incoming missiles during the Persian Gulf War in 1991.

Glossary

biomimicry (bye-oh-MI-mi-kree) the practice of copying nature in order to build or improve something

broadcast (BRAWD-kast) to send out radio or television signals

echolocation (ek-oh-lo-KAY-shuhn) a type of sonar used by bats, whales, and other animals

mammals (MAM-uhlz) warm-blooded animals that have hair or fur and give birth to live babies

nocturnal (nahk-TUR-nuhl) active mainly at night

patent (PAT-int) the legal ownership of an invention

prey (PRAY) an animal that is hunted by another animal for food

radar (RAY-dar) a way of finding objects by reflecting radio waves off them and receiving back the reflected waves

radio waves (RAY-dee-oh WAYVZ) amounts of energy that travel through air or water in the shape of a wave

reflected (ri-FLEK-tid) bounced off an object

sonar (SOH-nar) a way of finding objects by reflecting sound waves off them and receiving back the reflected waves

sound waves (SOUND WAYVZ) waves or series of vibrations

species (SPEE-sheez) groups of similar animals that are able to mate and have offspring with one another

For More Information

BOOKS

Carson, Mary Kay. *The Bat Scientists*. Boston: Houghton Mifflin, 2010.

Fleisher, Paul. *Doppler Radar, Satellites, and Computer Models: The Science of Weather Forecasting*. Minneapolis: Lerner Publications, 2011.

Spilsbury, Louise, and Richard Spilsbury. *The Radio*. Chicago: Heinemann Library, 2012.

WEB SITES

HowStuffWorks—How Radar Works
http://science.howstuffworks.com/radar.htm
Learn more about how radar works.

The Weather Channel—Interactive Weather Map
www.weather.com/weather/map/interactive
Enter your zip code to see what weather radars are showing in your area.

Index

airplanes, 5, 15-17, 19, 22, 26, 29
Appleton, Sir Edward V., 19

biomimicry, 23-24
bumblebee bats, 10

echoes, 4, 5-6, 11, 12, 15
echolocation, 11-12

flying fox bats, 10

Hertz, Heinrich, 6, 14
Hyland, Lawrence A., 26, 29

ionosphere, 19

Marconi, Guglielmo, 15

patents, 19, 26, 29
Persian Gulf War, 29

radio waves, 4-6, 14-15, 16, 19
Rines, Robert H., 26, 29

safety, 22
sound waves, 6-7, 8, 11-12, 16
space exploration, 22-23
submarines, 7-8, 22, 26

Tesla, Nikola, 25-26

U.S. Naval Research Laboratory (NRL), 15-16, 26

Watson-Watt, Sir Robert Alexander, 19
weather, 5, 15, 22
word origins, 4, 6
World War II, 6, 16, 20-21, 22, 29

About the Author

Josh Gregory writes and edits books for kids. He lives in Chicago, Illinois.